Library of Congress Cataloging-in-Publication Data
Cech, John.
The elves and the shoemaker / retold by John Cech ; illustrated by Kirill Chelushkin.
p. cm.
Summary: A poor shoemaker becomes successful with the help
of two elves who finish his shoes during the night.
ISBN-13: 978-1-4027-3067-2
ISBN-10: 1-4027-3067-5
[1. Fairy tales. 2. Folklore—Germany.] I. Chelushkin, Kirill, ill. II.
Grimm, Jacob, 1785–1863. III. Grimm, Wilhelm, 1786–1859. IV.
Elves and the shoemaker. English. V. Title.

PZ8.C293El 2007

398.2—dc22   2006006594

2 4 6 8 10 9 7 5 3 1

Published by Sterling Publishing Co., Inc.
387 Park Avenue South, New York, NY 10016
Text © 2007 by John Cech
Illustrations © 2007 by Kirill Chelushkin
Distributed in Canada by Sterling Publishing
c/o Canadian Manda Group, 165 Dufferin Street,
Toronto, Ontario, Canada M6K 3H6
Distributed in the United Kingdom by GMC Distribution Services,
Castle Place, 166 High Street, Lewes, East Sussex, England BN7 1XU
Distributed in Australia by Capricorn Link (Australia) Pty. Ltd.
P.O. Box 704, Windsor, NSW 2756, Australia

Design by Josh Simons, Simonsays Design!

Sterling ISBN-13: 978-1-4027-3067-2
ISBN-10: 1-4027-3067-5

For information about custom editions, special sales, premium and
corporate purchases, please contact Sterling Special Sales
Department at 800-805-5489 or specialsales@sterlingpub.com

THE CLASSIC
FAIRY TALE COLLECTION

The Elves and the Shoemaker

Retold by John Cech
Illustrated by Kirill Chelushkin

Sterling Publishing Co., Inc.
New York

For my grandson, Jage, who knows (truly, deeply) how
to cobble together those daily miracles of the imagination.

—J.C.

A long, long time ago, when shoes were still made by shoemakers and not by machines in factories, a shoemaker and his wife found themselves in very hard times. No matter how much they worked—and they worked hard indeed—they just couldn't seem to get ahead.

Things became so difficult that finally the shoemaker had only one piece of leather left—just enough to make one pair of shoes.

That evening, he cut out the pieces for the shoes he was going to stitch together the next morning. Walking to his bed, he thought to himself, "All we can do now is hope for the best."

When the shoemaker stepped into his workroom the next morning, he found the shoes all sewn together and neatly placed side by side on his workbench. The shoes were marvelous. Everything about them was perfect.

"I wonder who could have done this," the shoemaker said to his wife. But neither of them had heard a sound in the night.

oon the bell to their shop door rang, and in came a customer who looked at the shoes, tried them on, and said that no shoes had ever fit him so well. He happily gave the shoemaker twice the price he was asking for the shoes, and with the money the shoemaker bought enough leather for two more pairs of shoes.

That evening the shoemaker again cut out the pieces of leather, left them on his workbench, and then went to bed.

The next morning, two bright new pairs of shoes lay finished on his table. Soon they were sold as well.

This time the shoemaker bought enough leather to make
four pairs of shoes, which, like the others, were made overnight.
By now the whole town had begun to buzz about the shoemaker's
exceptional shoes, and all four pairs were quickly bought.

And so it went for weeks and months and into the cold winter. The shoemaker and his wife were busy all the time now. They worked so hard they barely had time to think.

One day the shoemaker said to his wife, "Let's stay up tonight and see who is doing this wonderful thing for us."

They hid themselves in the back of the shop and waited and waited and waited. But eventually they dozed off.

Suddenly the shoemaker and his wife were awakened by the sound of tapping. They rubbed their eyes in amazement to see two tiny, barefoot elves, dressed in thin, frayed red suits, deftly sewing the shoes together and tapping on the soles.

The elves finished their work, lined up the shoes on the bench, and left the shoemaker's shop like two whispers in the wind.

The shoemaker's wife looked at her husband and said, "Their little suits are so thin and tattered. They must be freezing. I'll make them little jackets, scarves, and hats, and you can cobble some shoes for them. It's the least that we can do to thank them."

So the shoemaker's wife made each of the elves a smart little suit with tiny gold buttons, and scarves and hats of the softest wool. And her husband made each of them a perfect pair of shoes.

That night they set the clothes out for the elves and waited. When the elves arrived just before daybreak, they looked at the little suits and began to dance with joy. They tried on their new clothes and admired each other, and then they sang:

We look so good, we look so smart—our cobbling days are done.

No more leather, no more thread—let's go out and have some fun!

And with that they danced out the door.

The shoemaker and his wife never saw the elves again, but good fortune had smiled on them and they became known across the land for their hard work, their wonderful shoes, and their kind souls.

Everyone has probably heard that the best solution when trying to solve a difficult problem is simply to "sleep on it." The belief that things will be put right while we're fast asleep is at least as old as the Brothers Grimm, who put this advice to the test in "The Elves and the Shoemaker." Although this story and others were first published by Jacob and Wilhelm Grimm in their 1812 collection of fairy tales called *Children's and Household Stories*, the brothers did not actually write the stories. Instead, they gathered the fairy tales from all over Germany, editing them into the versions that exist today.

The Grimms dedicated themselves to collecting these stories because they were afraid that they might be lost if they were not written down. One particularly rich source of stories were the Grimms' next door neighbors, the Wild family, who provided Jacob and Wilhelm with a number of their best-known tales. From Dortchen Wild, who would later marry Wilhelm, the Brothers Grimm learned three fairy tales about elves, the most famous of which remains with us today as "The Elves and the Shoemaker."

In this tale, the Grimms provided a glimpse of the ancient belief that small but powerful forces are at work in the world. Among the magical inhabitants of Northern Europe and the British Isles were a group of creatures collectively referred to as elves, although the legends, lore, names, and habits of these spirits varied widely from country to country.

Elves were generally believed to be small, playful tricksters who might either create problems or be remarkably helpful in the households that they chose to visit. In fact, it was very important that one reward the elves with a bowl of milk or porridge for the help they provided. If the elves were not rewarded, they might take offense and leave a disaster in their wake, like giving the sleepers in the house nightmares (which in German translates literally as "elf dreams"). One should be sure, however, never to present the elves with a gift of clothing (as the shoemaker and his wife do in this tale), or else they would disappear, never to return.

There have been many retellings of "The Elves and the Shoemaker" since the Grimms first published their fairy tale, including a recent version of the story that takes place in the American Wild West. One traditional tale from Cornwall, in the far west of England, tells of an elf (known there as a piskey) who secretly helps an elderly couple with the chores on their farm each night while they are asleep. When they discover who their helper is, the old woman decides to thank the piskey by making him a new suit of clothes, despite the warnings of the old man. He tells his wife that the clothes will lead the piskey to think that the couple is spying on him. He'll be offended and vanish—which is exactly what happens.

The continued presence in today's world of "The Elves and the Shoemaker," as well as other fairy tales by the Brothers Grimm, illustrates how right Wilhelm and Jacob were about the importance of preserving these tales. In fact, when asked what books children should read, world-renowned physicist Albert Einstein reportedly replied, "If you want your children to be intelligent, read them fairy tales. If you want them to be more intelligent, read them more fairy tales."